This Book Belongs To:

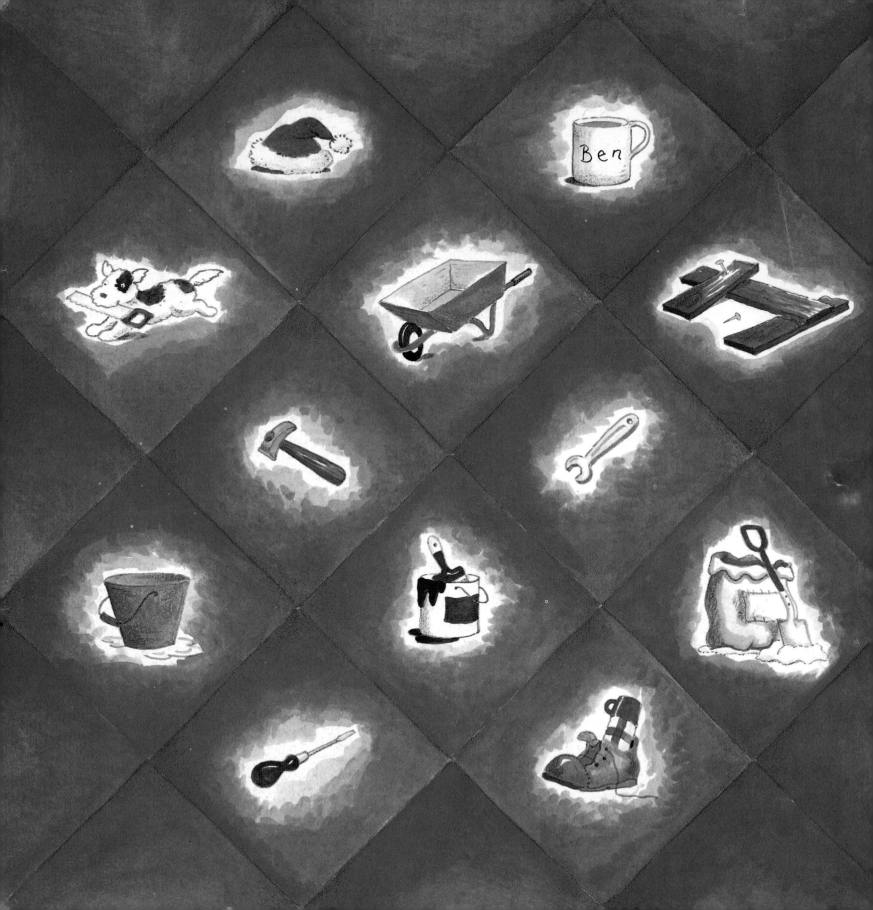

This is a Bright Sparks Book
First published in 2001

Bright Sparks
Queen Street House
4 Queen Street
Bath BA1 1HE, UK

This book was created by
small world creations ltd
25a Long Street, Tetbury, GL8 8AA, UK

Written by Ronne Randall
Illustrated by Frank Endersby

Benny the Bumbling Builder

Bright ☆ Sparks

Benny was a hard-working builder, and he always did his **very best**.
But sometimes he could be **forgetful**!
One morning, Benny the Builder arrived bright and early
at Vet Vicky's surgery.

"Benny the Builder
at your service!"   he announced.
"I think you have a job for me to do."

"Not today, Benny," replied Vicky. "But Polly the Postlady is expecting you!"
"Of course!" said Benny. "Sorry - I really shouldn't be so forgetful!"
And off he went to Polly the Postlady's house.

"Benny the Builder at your service!" Benny announced.
"Woof!" said Benny's dog, Rocky.

"Come in,"
called Polly.

She took out a drawing to show Benny.
"I want you to build a **Wendy house** in my garden." Polly said.
"It's a **surprise** for my grandchildren, Peter, Penny and Patty.
I did this drawing to show you just how it should look."

Benny and Polly looked at the drawing together.

"The Wendy house should have two tall doors," said Polly,
"one at the front and one at the back, with one small step at the back door.

"Yes, I see,"

said Benny.

"There should be **five windows**," said Polly,
"one at either side of the front door
and one on each of the other sides."

"Yes, I see," said Benny.
'And I want a nice **sloping roof**," said Polly, "not a **flat roof**!"
"Yes, I see," said Benny. "I will do my **very best**!"

Polly left for the post office, and Benny
went out to start work. But he had barely
begun when a gust of wind came along.

WHOOSH! went Polly's drawing, up in the air.

WHOOSH!

"WOOF!" barked Rocky, leaping up to catch it.
Oh no!
The drawing got caught in the branches of a tree!

Rocky fetched the drawing but, by the time
Benny got it back, it was in shreds.

"Oh dear!" moaned Benny the Builder.
"How will I build the Wendy House now?"

Benny tried to remember everything in the drawing. But he quickly got very confused!

"Was it five windows and two doors with one step?" Benny puzzled.

Benny decided that he would just have to do the best he could.

He got to work measuring...
mixing...laying bricks...

...sawing wood...
...hammering nails...

...fixing screws...
...plastering and painting...

...and doing his very **best** to make everything just right.

Late that afternoon, Postlady Polly got home from work.

She couldn't wait to see what Benny had done.
But, what a **surprise** she had!

The Wendy house's roof was **flat**.
The bottom of the house was **sloping**.
There were **two steps** leading up to **two doors on one side** of the house.

There were two floors, both different sizes.
And there were two windows on one side of the house.

"It's all wrong!" said Polly to Benny. "How will you ever fix it in time?"

Benny didn't have a chance to answer, because just then, Polly's grandchildren arrived.

"Look! A Wendy house!"
they cried happily, rushing towards it.

"There's a door for each of us!" they all cried together.
"And we can climb right up to the roof!" said Patty.

"And slide down the other side!" said Peter.
"And there are loads of windows so it's nice and bright inside!" said Penny.

"**Granny**, it's the **best** Wendy house ever!" the children told Polly.
"Thank you so much!"

"Well, I think you should thank Benny the Builder,"
said Postlady Polly smiling.

Benny the Builder smiled too. "I just did my very best," he said.